T0208114

ALPHA SPIES

THE RISE OF OCEANUS

CHARITY TEH

For book orders, email orders@traffordpublishing.com.sg

Most Trafford Singapore titles are also available at major online book retailers.

Printed in Singapore.

ISBN: 978-1-4669-2821-3 (sc)
ISBN: 978-1-4669-2822-0 (hc)
ISBN: 978-1-4669-2823-7 (e)

Trafford rev. 11/09/2012

 www.traffordpublishing.com.sg

Singapore
toll-free: 800 101 2656 (Singapore)
Fax: 800 101 2656 (Singapore)

Chapter 1

Kyle Robinson was in a good mood today. He made the teacher forget their homework by faking an entire act. That morning, he had fallen from the monkey bars, leaving crimson red scrapes on both of his hands. An idea sparked in his mind. If he made the teacher worried about his scrapes, she might forget his homework!

It was a success. Not only did the teacher forget his homework, but she got so mixed up that she gave everyone a holiday!

Kyle skipped back home with his twin sister Vickie happily. They burst into the door and raced upstairs to their room. Flopping down excitedly on their bed, they started to play on their Nintendo

Wii. But when they were just inserting the CD in the player . . .

The floor was shaking. Kyle and Vickie fell over each other. The television went black and a message flashed on its screen:

> Vickie and Kyle,
>
> You have been chosen for your special skills to join the Alpha Spies and go on your first training mission. We have been observing you and we have come to the conclusion that you are now capable of taking care of yourself. For more details, meet me at the park at midnight. Good luck.

Vickie gasped. Kyle's eyes grew big. They stared at the screen with their mouths hanging open.

"It must be just a prank." Vickie decided.

"I don't think so." Kyle considered for a moment. "Pranksters don't talk that way."

"We'd better go to bed early then." Vickie muttered eagerly. "Midnights are VERY late for me."

That night, Kyle couldn't sleep. He twisted and turned but he was still awake. He checked his alarm clock. 11:59. Just one more minute . . .

Vickie was wide awake. She stared at the ceiling, wondering what would happen if someone had tricked them. Glancing at the clock, she read the time.

12:00.

Kyle grabbed his iPad and Vickie brought an ultraviolet flashlight. Creeping silently across the squeaky wooden corridor, they tiptoed outside and ran all the way to the park.

Vickie shone her flashlight around. Nobody was there.

"It was just a joke after all." Kyle said disappointedly.

A twig snapped behind them. Whirling around, Kyle and Vickie turned around to see a tall, red haired woman about 20 years old.

"Hello, Vickie! Hi, Kyle!" she grinned. "I'm Janie. I sent you the message."

"But what is our mission?" Kyle wondered.

"You have to defeat Oceanus." Janie replied. "He is one of the most powerful people on earth."

"Wow." Vickie was taken aback by this reply. "So, is he like Poseidon or something?"

"Nope. He just calls himself Oceanus because he is a great swimmer and he can charm fish. And that's all he can do!"

"Ok, so WHERE is he?" Kyle muttered.

"Hi, I'm Janie. I sent you the message."

"Our villain radar shows that he is somewhere in Australia." Janie shrugged. "I know it's a big place, but you are the only one that can save the world."

Vickie took a deep breath. "I'm doing it, Kyle." She smiled. "A team's gotta do what a team's gotta do."

"So this is where WE are helpful!" Kyle exclaimed. "I'm in!"

"Right," Janie grinned. "Let's do this!"

Chapter 2

"Here are your flight tickets." Janie pulled two crumpled looking bits of card out of her backpack. "I'll go with you, so I'll just pretend to be your mum or something."

Vickie took the tickets and put them in her pocket. "But what would our mum say?"

"Hmm . . . good point. We'll have to tell her that you're going on a field trip to a very faraway country like America or Argentina." Janie said. "She'll probably understand."

"Bye then." Kyle smiled.

They trooped off into the darkness.

Oceanus was sipping a glass of wine when his servants, Maris and L'ocèan burst into the door.

"What now?" Oceanus muttered.

Maris nearly tripped over her long, white dress when she heard her master speak.

"E-err your M-majesty, the Alpha Spies h-have r-recruited a new team of s-spies!" she stammered. "What should we do?

"Do?" Oceanus rippled with laughter. "We won't do anything! They won't find ME here!"

He shoved a bunch of purple grapes in his mouth, grinning.

L'ocèan was still discouraged. "But, your Majesty, they've-"

"I don't care what they did!" Oceanus snarled furiously, knocking over his dinner table. "If you want to DO something, go and tell my soldiers to capture them!"

"Yes, your Majesty!" They scurried outside.

Oceanus rippled with laughter.

Oceanus smiled. Some day, he would take over the whole world . . .

Meanwhile, Kyle and Vickie were lying on their front porch in the hot sunshine.

"I wonder why it was US that were chosen." Vickie said.

"Well, it was our 'special skills' that did it." Kyle replied thoughtfully. "But I wonder what they are."

"Well, I'm good at spying and you're good at climbing." Vickie decided. "But still, WHY us?"

"I don't know." Kyle muttered. "They've been spying on us for ages now, so I guess we'll have to wait and see."

Janie arrived, wearing a bright pink sweatshirt and jeans. She parked her Mercedes and Kyle and Vickie climbed in.

"Ok, then." She grinned. "Let's get to Australia!"

Chapter 3

The Mercedes swerved to a halt. The bustling airport was full of businessmen, university students and foreigners.

"Ok then." Janie leapt out of the car and let out a gasp of relief. "I hope we catch this aeroplane on time."

Stopping only to buy a supply of chocolate bars, soda and mints, they raced to the plane just before take off. The stewardess glanced at them sternly.

"Where are your parents?" she asked Janie.

"Dead," Janie replied. "We were sent here by my parents' employers."

When the stewardess went to see another passenger, Kyle muttered under his breath, "Janie,

The Mercedes swerved to a halt.

why did you lie? She could have sent us to Social Services."

"I told her the truth." Janie gulped silently. "My parents were murdered by Oceanus, and we were sent here by their employers; the Alpha Spies."

"Ohhh." Vickie mouth turned into a perfect circle. "So, how did Oceanus kill them? I mean, they must have had bodyguards with guns and stuff!"

"They did." Janie replied. "But Oceanus's pet crabs bit them to death."

There was silence. Kyle imagined being bitten to death. It seemed so horrible—so cruel. It WAS horrible and cruel.

"Excuse me, but would you like Coke or coffee with your curry?" A different stewardess smiled at them politely. They all wanted Coke, and a minute later three steaming trays arrived with ice-cold Cokes perched next to them arrived at their table. Kyle slurped happily, forgetting the gruesome fact that he had just imagined.

"You've got Coke on your nose!" Vickie laughed. She pulled out her UV flashlight and began to play with it thoughtfully. She shone it at her table and gasped. There was a hidden message scrawled on it:

> To Australia you must go,
> But where? Nobody knows.
> The only thing that I can say,
> Near a beach is where you'll stay.
> Ends with H, starts with P,
> You probably know where I mean.

Vickie smiled. "Perth!"

"Cool!" Kyle yelled. "We get to build sandcastles!"

Janie rolled her eyes. "Oceanus was born in Perth." she said. "But who would send a message like that?"

Vickie shrugged. "Dunno."

"Maybe it's an anonymous friend." Kyle said.

The plane landed. They were in Australia at last.

Chapter 4

Kyle snatched up his iPad and took a picture of the doodled message. There might be some more hidden clues there, he thought.

Janie was shaking the bags down from their compartments when a startling mew squealed from Vickie's rucksack. A small, shivering kitten was struggling out of the bag. Kyle gasped.

"How did he get here?" Vickie wondered.

"She," Janie smiled. "Ginger is a she."

"Ginger?"

The bright orange kitten stared up at them. Then she began to sniff the ground. She could see a lot of people, and people meant food, and food meant only one thing: FISH.

The bright orange kitten stared up at them.

With a pounce she leapt onto a little girl and began to search her pockets like a little police-cat. Unfortunately, the girl was allergic to cats. She sneezed so loudly, that it caught the attention of all the cabin crew; including the grumpy stewardess. She stormed to Janie with a face that looked like Thunder.

"This is all your doing, I know," she hissed at Janie. "First you come aboard my flight with absolutely NO supervision, and now you let loose a kitten on board. Security!"

They turned to run, but policemen with guns started towards them. Janie picked up Ginger and pressed a button on her collar. Bullets started shooting out, blowing the police away like pollen.

"I knew that would work!" Janie grinned at the stunned stewardess. "Come on, we'd better get out of here!"

They ran out, treading on the stewardess's toe as they went.

Kyle sat in the taxi petting Ginger. They had to get to Perth before the police did.

"Even if they put us in jail," Vickie thought, "I think we should be Ok because I heard from a friend that jails in Australia are *luxurious!!*"

"Um, that's just impossible." Kyle muttered. "That's just persuading people to be murderers."

Janie nodded. "That's exactly why Oceanus wanted to be the bad guy. He just wanted more free ice-cream!"

Then Kyle remembered something. "Janie, why was it us that were chosen for this mission?"

Janie smiled. "You two have hidden skills. They should be revealed at the end of this mission."

"That's a long time." Vickie sighed.

The taxi swerved to a halt. They were in Perth at last.

Chapter 5

Vickie stared at Kyle's iPad. The poem, still in its purplish form even after Kyle had spilt curry all over it just after the plane had landed, was written as if the person who wrote it was in a hurry.

Then she noticed something. There were dots on top of some of the letters. It must be a code, she thought.

To Australia you must go,
But where? Nobody knows.
The only thing that I can say,
Near a beach is where you'll stay.
Ends with H, starts with P,
You probably know where I mean

She put the dotted letters together.

HIDE.

Hide?

But . . . who would want them to hide?

She listed them in her mind. Not Oceanus. Not Janie. Janie was *helping* them to hide.

Kyle bent over what she was doing, casting a shadow over the message.

"Kyle! I've found a code!"

Kyle read the word she wrote on her notepad. "Hide?" he muttered. "We're already hiding from Oceanus."

"Maybe. But there is a possibility that Oceanus is in this airport, so maybe he's watching us now!"

They glanced around nervously. Only Janie was there, asking a policeman for directions.

Then Vickie saw a glint of metal slide from the policeman's hand into Kyle's backpack. She raised her eyebrows and unzipped the backpack cautiously.

A red beam shone straight at her face, nearly blinding her. She could hear a clock beeping. Was it a bomb?

She snatched up the grenade and smashed it onto the floor. The metal pieces chimed one more time, then stopped. The bomb was broken.

The bomb was broken.

Chapter 6

Kyle picked up a shattered piece of the bomb and studied it carefully. A green bit of cardboard fell out and Vickie caught it in mid-air.

"Who would put a bit of cardboard in a bomb?" Janie said.

Vickie shrugged. "Maybe the bomb wasn't a real bomb. Maybe it was supposed to push out the cardboard when the clock stops beeping."

"But who was the policeman?" Kyle asked. "No random policeman drops fake bombs in kids' backpacks!"

Vickie glanced at the card again. There was writing on it, but it was all gibberish.

2|1 Fake

MRAEIEPFT FMRUE SAHPT

ZGKTAOTJAE 10.

-DA TSFYRGKIBEJLNGD

"Ok, now what does that mean?" Kyle muttered.

"I think I know what to do to crack the code," Janie smiled. "You have to take the first letter, 'M', which is the first letter of the decoded message. Then skip two fake letters, 'R' and 'A', so the next letter in the message is 'E'!"

"So we have to skip one letter after that and so on?" Vickie exclaimed. "Ok, that's easy!"

After lots of scribbling and rubbing out, the decoded message was finally revealed.

MEET ME AT GATE 10.

-A FRIEND

"That took a long time." Kyle sighed, wiping a gland of sweat from his forehead.

"But nobody else knows that we're on this mission other than the Alpha Spies staff." Vickie said. "So who do we have to meet?"

Reaching for the backpacks (and Ginger), they headed to Gate 10.

L'ocèan was exhausted. First, he had to escape from Oceanus's guards as he was getting out of the castle. Then, he had to devise and edit a brand new code. After that, he had to phone the Alpha Spies' grumpy manager that he had arrived at Gate 10.

After all, he was a secret agent.

A very tired secret agent.

He wondered if he could take a quick nap. It would only be for a few minutes, he thought to himself.

But what if they came? He would have to be awake then.

A little snooze wouldn't do any harm, he concluded. Lying on a bench, he slowly drifted off to sleep.

Lying on a bench, he slowly drifted off to sleep.

Chapter 7

Vickie, Kyle and Janie trooped across to Gate 10. It was empty. Only a snoring beggar covered in rags was there.

"All right, now what?" Vickie muttered.

Kyle shrugged. "Maybe the beggar is the friend..."

"No way! How could a beggar be a spy?" Vickie yelled exasperatedly.

"He could be." Janie replied. "Look at the watch on his arm. That's not even a watch, it's a computerized teleporter!"

They gasped. The figure began to rub his eyes. Sitting up rapidly, he stared at them with bulging eyes.

"Hi, my name is L'ocèan. I'm a secret agent for the Alpha Spies, disguised as Oceanus's servant. My real name is Reuben, but Oceanus changed it after he kidnapped me when I was a toddler."

Kyle shifted uncomfortably. "So, you sent us that message?"

"The policeman who dropped the bomb in your backpack was actually my sister Maris in disguise." Reuben replied. "Her real name is Minerva, named after the Greek goddess of wisdom. Oceanus had that changed as well."

"We're sorry we called you a beggar," Vickie said, but Reuben cut her off in mid-sentence.

"I am a beggar." He replied. "Oceanus took away all our money, including the gold locket that my mother gave Minerva."

"I need your help." He added. "That locket is the most powerful thing in history, but Oceanus doesn't know that yet. We need to get it back, and fast."

There was a long silence.

"We'll do it." Kyle replied, stepping forward. "We'll help you find that locket."

Reuben beamed happily. "Let's go!"

Reuben beamed happily. "Let's go!"

Chapter 8

Reuben pressed a button on his teleporter. A purple coloured tube appeared in the middle of the busy airport. Nobody else seemed to notice even though the tube was shining as if its life depended on it.

"Step inside," Reuben said. "You'll be immediately transported to my underwater spy room."

"Cool!" Kyle was the first to step inside. As he went in, he gave a squeal of delight as the purple tube sucked him in.

"Me next." Vickie jumped inside. But the tube began to malfunction and Vickie's joyful face turned the colour of ash.

"Run!" Janie grabbed Vickie's shoulder and pulled with all her strength. But it was too late.

The tube was dissolving. Vickie screamed but it was no use. She disappeared into thin air and everything went black.

Light began to gleam through Vickie's eyelids. Where was she?

She sat up. She was sitting on solid rock. But where was Kyle?

Kyle appeared, wearing a shimmering black spy outfit. "Vickie, check this out!" He grinned. "This jacket has got my name on it!"

"Then I bet there's one for me too!" Vickie followed Kyle into the closet, and she saw a glimmering fluorescent outfit waiting for her.

"No fair! Yours is much better than mine!" Kyle argued.

Vickie laughed. Never before had she got the better item than Kyle.

"Where's Janie?" Kyle asked. Vickie began to pour out the story of the tragedy.

"So, we're stuck underground with no food. I am definitely going to miss macaroni cheese." Kyle sighed.

"Come on, Kyle, there has to be some food somewhere." Vickie got up and started searching the cupboards. No food.

"Well, I'm going to miss lemonade." Vickie was going to sit down again when she noticed a trapdoor. Bending down to examine it, she saw a keypad.

A code!

She was good at these.

She pressed a button that said 'hint' and read what it said:

FIRST AUTHOR OF THE 39 CLUES

She thought back. Way back, when Vickie and Kyle were 8. The 39 Clues was their favourite book.

Peter Lerangis? No, he wrote Book 7. Gordon Korman? No, he wrote Book 2. Rick Riordan?

Bending down to examine it, she saw a keypad.

He was the first author!

She typed in the answer.

The trapdoor opened to reveal a hidden staircase. Vickie shone her ultraviolet light to the bottom of the steps and gasped. At the bottom of the staircase was food.

Kyle raced over to her. "I smelt burgers." He grinned. They sprinted to the bottom of the staircase.

Cupboards were laden with pizza, macaroni and at least 10 different types of cheese.

Kyle reached for the nearest can of Coke and slurped it happily. Then he began to feel dizzy. He swayed to the ground and blacked out.

Chapter 9

Vickie was still scanning the spaghetti when she heard the crash.

She whirled around. Kyle was lying on the floor unconscious. The can of Coke was dripping onto the rickety floorboards.

Was there poison in the Coke? Had Kyle been drugged?

Before she could think the question over, a laser ray glinted from the ceiling. A hole appeared in the ground just below Kyle. Kyle dropped down, down, down . . .

Was there poison in the Coke?

Never before had Vickie been so scared. She remembered the moment when their mom told them that they could go on the 'field trip'.

"Take care of your brother," she had said. Even though Vickie and Kyle were twins, Vickie was 26 seconds older. To Vickie, those 26 seconds counted a lot.

With shaking hands, Vickie took the can of Coke and dropped in down the hole. 10 seconds of clinking and clanking later, the can ground to a halt.

Vickie was petrified. She took a grappling hook and fastened one end to a cupboard handle, one end on her belt. Carefully, she lowered herself down into the endless pit.

After a few minutes, Vickie was exhausted. She must be about 50 metres down by now, she muttered. That's when she felt the pulling sensation on her left ankle.

She glanced down. It was Kyle!

"Where have you been?" she cried. Then she realized the barrel of the gun pointing at her.

"Kyle," Vickie was confused. "What's going on?"

Kyle squeezed the trigger. A piercing dart soared into the air, and then landed.

Vickie screamed in agony. The dart stopped vibrating. She could feel a trickle of liquid flowing down her arm.

Everything went black.

Vickie woke up. A faint glimmer of light shone through her eyelids. She sat up.

She was in a lab. Test tubes were scattered around the room. Lasers blocked the windows and doors. If only she could turn them off . . .

She felt too tired to do anything. In reply to this thought, she drifted off to sleep.

Chapter 10

Vickie woke up. Two men in black were in the room, rummaging through her backpack. Vickie didn't care. All they would find would be a boring book, a battered up iPhone and . . .

Her ultraviolet light.

She sprang out of her bed. Nobody else knew, but that UV light doubled as a plasma beam. The men in black were startled and started shooting at her. Vickie dodged the bullets easily. Then she noticed that the men in black had left the lasers off. She grabbed her backpack and sprinted for the door.

She raced out of the door. Squinting to see the sign, she gasped.

Oceanus Inc.

Oceanus had started a company? Vickie was confused. She tried to think of something else. She thought of her geography homework.

She had to write a four-page report on Oceania. That just made it worse.

She collapsed. It seemed that Oceanus had taken over her life, her mind, her brother. Even her geography homework was related to Oceanus.

She had to rescue Kyle.

But what about herself? She could get fried by plasma beams before she even got to the door.

"Take care of your brother," the voice rang into her ears again.

She had to do it.

But not now. She had to get some rest.

She saw a bush. It wasn't as prickly as the others. Maybe she could sleep there, she thought.

She stepped in. Then she realized something. She was teetering on the edge of a giant hole. She lost her balance.

She was teetering on the edge of a giant hole.

She fell, fell, and fell . . .

She was dazed. Straining to see around her, she could make out a figure. He was sitting on a pod chair, playing what looked like a Nintendo DS.

"Kyle!"

The boy didn't hear her.

Vickie grabbed the Nintendo DS and threw it on the floor. The boy looked up at her. It was Kyle. Or at least, looked like Kyle.

She felt 'Kyle's' arm. It wasn't skin. Only cold, icy metal.

A robot!

She backed away in panic. The robot raised his hand. From behind Vickie, a bullet was being fired. She crumpled to the ground with only one scream.

Kyle.

Chapter 11

Kyle rubbed his eyes. He was in a soft bed covered in blankets. He must be home now, he thought. It was all just a dream. Janie was a dream, Oceanus was a dream. It was just a nightmare.

Then he noticed the scientific equipment around the room and remembered what had happened. Oceanus had told his personal scientists to make an exact replica of him into a robot.

It wasn't a dream.

He wondered what Vickie was doing now. Probably still looking at more cheeseburgers. What a responsible sister, he muttered sarcastically.

He tried to move closer to the edge of the bed without security cameras spotting him. But his leg was so excruciatingly painful that he couldn't move an inch without yelling in agony. The door handle was moving and he shut his eyes quickly.

No lasers were shining at him, no guns were pointing at his head.

Only a bedraggled kitten stared up at him, mewing in concern.

"Ginger?"

Then it all came back to him. Before he was sucked into the teleporting machine, Ginger had crept into his backpack and went to sleep.

"But—how did you open the door?"

He imagined what Ginger was thinking in his mind:

Of course it's me, you strange humanoid. Remember my collar? The bulletproof, spiked collar with 5 barrels of ammunition and a built in webcam that doubles as an ultrasound recorder? Yes, that collar. Well it has an equally powerful robotic hand that can reach up to any height AND CAN OPEN DOORS! You humanoids should remember what you invented.

Kyle shook his head, trying to get the voice out of his mind. But he couldn't.

When you were born, the Alpha Spies specially implanted a microchip in your brain to hear what I think. Your parents were furious and forbid you to enter anything to do with spies. But the Alpha Spies needed you for this mission.

"Whoa." Kyle was stunned.

On my way here, I saw a gold locket in a glass case. It looks like Minerva's. My built in radar tells me that Vickie is unconscious. Choose what you want to do first. Save your sister—or save the world from Oceanus's power.

Kyle was placed into a dilemma. He had to save his sister. But the world would be at the mercy of Oceanus if he did that.

Well, he couldn't overpower Oceanus if he didn't work with Vickie, he thought. He had to rescue Vickie.

"I'll go get Vickie." he said to the cat, smiling.

"On my way here, I saw a gold locket in a glass case. It looks like Minerva's."

Chapter 12

Reuben tapped the teleporter. The only thing that happened was the purple energy swirling inside it.

"Great. Just great. Now they are trapped and it's my mission to NOT get them trapped!" Janie yelled furiously. "The Alpha Spies are going to kill me."

"We have to get them back somehow." Minerva said nervously. "Oceanus is probably on their trail already."

"Yeah. And this time, the microchip had better work!" Janie sat down exasperatedly. "But what use is a talking cat?"

Reuben tried to calm her down. "We could always send another cat to help," he reasoned. "I have invented an electronic cat that can talk and decode messages in a millisecond . . ."

"I don't care!" Janie hollered. "Who cares about technology? Especially *cats*. If a person nearby was allergic to cat fur, Ginger would have to be shipped out of the town! That's not going to help anybody, is it?"

Meanwhile, at Oceanus Inc., a boy could be seen walking through the corridors. But this boy was not Kyle.

In fact, this was Oceanus's own son, Aiden. He was a secret agent for the Alpha Spies, but of course, Oceanus didn't know that.

His eyes glanced at the gold locket encased in the glass. He had to get it or the Alpha Spies would kick him out of the mission. That's when he heard the alarm.

People were scrambling all around the room with fire extinguishers but only Aiden knew the real reason to the alarm.

After all, he was the only one who bothered to look at the security camera videos.

He ran towards the tech lab and put a very confused Kyle and Ginger on a stretcher. Kyle was yelling at him but Ginger was calm. Ginger knew that Aiden was part of the Alpha Spies mission.

Aiden sprinted to his bike and pressed a hidden button underneath the saddle. The bike immediately transformed into a hovercraft.

He pushed Kyle and Ginger inside and onto a passenger seat. He could hear the screams below shouting, "Traitor!"

He didn't care. But how was he going to get the locket?

Kyle was becoming quiet now. "Thanks for saving me, but who are you?"

"I'm Aiden, Oceanus's son." Aiden replied. "I'm a secret agent for the Alpha Spies."

So many people are secret agents nowadays, Kyle thought. "Now how are we going to get Minerva's locket?"

"Well, we'd better find Vickie first." Aiden said. He pushed a button and the hovercraft blasted away.

"I'm Aiden, Oceanus's son."

Chapter 13

Oceanus grinned. He had captured the Alpha Spies agents, found Minerva's locket and his son was graduating the very next day.

He decided to go to Aiden's bedroom to congratulate him. He walked to the other side of the building and opened the door, only to see a messy bed and the radio blaring out music at high volume.

He scowled. Where was Aiden when you needed him?

Then he noticed the figure beside him. His servant was puffing and panting as he had run all the way from the servant apartments to Oceanus's house.

"What now?" Oceanus glared at the servant.

"The hovercraft has been stolen, your Majesty." The servant shifted his feet uncomfortably. "It was unlocked at precisely 3: 39: 15, exactly the time when the alarm sounded."

Oceanus was furious. "AIDEN!"

Minerva sighed. She wondered what sort of 'scientific experiments' was Reuben doing now.

She glanced at her burger silently. It was a double cheeseburger, and it cost 2 dollars 50 cents. But when the receipt came, she was confused. The receipt said that her burger was a lot more than 2.50.

Perhaps it's a code, she thought. She pulled out a pen and began to decipher the message slowly.

Perhaps it's a code, she
thought.

RECEIPT

CODE NUMBER P4GR492CXP

DOUBLE CHEESEBURGER: 23.00

COKE: 5.00

COLESLAW: 1.00

VEGGIE BURGER: 18.00

COKE: 5.00

COFFEE: 15.00

FRENCH FRIES: 11.00

Minerva, after a few minutes, managed to write the message on a piece of paper.

WE ARE OK

Minerva smiled, ignoring the explosion caused by Reuben's chemical. She knew recruiting Aiden was a good idea. Aiden was an expert cryptographer, an expert on poisons, and of course, an expert back-stabber.

She grinned again. Oceanus, hopefully, hadn't found out, but even if he did, Aiden would be able to escape with Kyle, Ginger, and possibly her locket.

She, of course, was an expert double agent.

Vickie's head hurt. Her heart was throbbing with the same rhythm as her head, which just made the pain worse.

She struggled to see the calendar on her bedside table. She had been here in the hospital for nearly a week now. She tried to remember the events since her life was changed by the Alpha Spies.

School, monkey bar scrapes, mad teacher.

She wished she'd stayed at home with her history homework.

She continued.

Message, Janie, recruited.

Her pain got worse.

She couldn't bear this any longer. Her chest was pounding so loud she could feel the noise bursting in her ears.

She closed her eyes. Maybe she was dead. Maybe she was abducted by aliens.

Abducted by aliens?

That was the exact thing Kyle would say.

Kyle couldn't function without her. She couldn't function without Kyle.

She ripped the blankets apart and waited for the alarm.

Chapter 14

Silence.

That was Kyle's least favourite sound in the world. He was lying in the hovercraft, waiting for something to happen. He didn't care what it was, as long as there was *something*.

He had been there for the past few hours doing nothing. He wondered how long it was since he had taken a bath. He counted on his fingers.

Five and a half days.

"Yuck."

Ginger's voice began ringing in his brain again.

So you think that's gross, huh? Well listen to this: My great-great-great—grand uncle's wife's mum's sister's son went on a hiking trip and a lion got him and blood

He had been there for the past few hours doing nothing.

splattered everywhere. And you still think five and a half days of grime is disgusting? I will never understand humans.

Kyle threw a pebble at Ginger. A satisfying yelp screamed in Kyle's head.

That really hurt, you repugnant humanoid. If I were a human I would call the cops on you!

"Yeah, but you're not a human. So what're you going to do now?" Kyle scowled at Ginger.

From the cockpit they could hear the radios blaring out at full volume.

Kyle was too exhausted to scold Ginger anymore. He closed his eyes and went to sleep.

No alarm.

Vickie lay back. She was worn out. She dug in her pockets for something to eat and found a half-melted chocolate bar, a stick of candy and a lollipop.

She tore the lollipop wrapper open and indulged herself into the taste of grape and strawberry. Her dream was burst when Oceanus crashed into the room.

"I may not be able to get Kyle, but you are going to be the first victim!" Oceanus raised his golden trident and pointed it at Vickie. A jet of water spurted out from the prongs and blasted Vickie in the face.

Then she heard a whirr of rotor blades. Kyle had come to rescue her at last.

Chapter 15

Kyle and Aiden bolted through the door and raced for Vickie but a sea of water blocked them and threw them to the floor. Vickie screamed and tried to break free but Oceanus's grip was firm. The trident pelted out more water and flooded the entire room. Vickie was still struggling but tiredness took over her and she lay still. Kyle gasped and swam to her side. Aiden used his own mini trident to hit Oceanus and it slammed into his face. Oceanus fell down and Ginger tied him up. Vickie was dragged out by Kyle who then smashed the case which held Minerva's locket. He grabbed it determinedly and raced out with Aiden and Ginger. Minerva and Reuben

Oceanus fell
down and Ginger
tied him up.

were waiting outside and they clambered into the hovercraft and let out a gasp of relief.

"Ok, we got the locket." Vickie said. "What do we do now?"

"Lock up the cat, I hope." Kyle groaned.

Minerva rolled her eyes. "Security will find Oceanus tied up in about less than an hour. If we go at maximum speed, they won't catch us in time."

"So what exactly is the locket supposed to do?" Kyle asked.

"When the wearer is in trouble, but only in *serious* trouble, the locket will grant one wish."

"Why don't you just wish to have infinity wishes?"

"There is a small list of exceptions." Reuben explained. "First, you can't wish for infinite things, such as wishes or even to drink the Elixir of Life. Second, you cannot put more than one wish into a full wish."

"What's that supposed to mean?" Vickie asked.

Minerva thought for a moment. "For example, you could be in a locked cage. You can't wish for the cage to unlock itself, the enemy not to find out and escape. That's a three in one."

"I get it." Kyle smiled. Vickie nodded too.

"But we won't really get to use it." Vickie said silently. "Our mission is over. We go home."

"Your mission isn't over yet." Aiden said. "This is only the beginning."

END OF BOOK ONE